Are you
crazy about
your pet?

and
cuddly
animals?

For budding
doctors and
nurses!

'The story mixes
lessons in safety
and first aid!'

Bo-Céleste, age 6

Perfect
for fans of
Holly Webb.

A note from the author:

Jane says . . .

'My first dog, Tinker, loved to swim in the river and then frisk around and roll in stinky mud. He always needed a bath when we got him home!'

There's a new swimming pool in Thistletown,
but what's wrong with Logan the puppy?
All his friends gather around him in the
changing room and wait for Dr KittyCat and
Peanut to come to the rescue!

Great Clarendon Street, Oxford OX2 6DP

Oxford University Press is a department of the University of Oxford.
It furthers the University's objective of excellence in research, scholarship,
and education by publishing worldwide

Oxford is a registered trade mark of Oxford University Press
in the UK and in certain other countries

Text © Jane Clarke and Oxford University Press 2018
Illustrations © Oxford University Press 2018

Cover artwork: Richard Byrne
Cover photograph: Eric Isselee/Shutterstock.com
Inside artwork: Dynamo
All animal images from Shutterstock
With thanks to Christopher Tancock for advising on the first aid

British Library Cataloguing in Publication Data

Data available

ISBN: 978-0-19-276598-7 (paperback)

2 4 6 8 10 9 7 5 3 1

Printed in China by Golden Cup
Paper used in the production of this book is a natural,
recyclable product made from wood grown in sustainable forests.
The manufacturing process conforms to the environmental
regulations of the country of origin.

Dr KittyCat

is ready to rescue

Logan the Puppy

Jane Clarke

OXFORD

UNIVERSITY PRESS

Chapter One

'Swim safe!' Peanut read out the words at the top of the new poster he was working on. 'No running in the pool area. No diving. No pushing. Never swim on your own. Listen to instructions . . .'

He turned to Dr KittyCat. She was busy knitting something that looked like a tiny pair of shorts with shoulder straps. Peanut's whiskers twitched.

Dr KittyCat was kind and caring and a wonderful furry first-aider, but Peanut wasn't a big fan of her knitting. *I hope that's not for me!* he thought.

'There's room for another line of writing on my poster,' Peanut told Dr KittyCat. 'What else is important for the little animals to know when they go to Thistletown's new swimming pool?'

Dr KittyCat put down her knitting and studied the poster.

'They should know where the safety equipment is,' she said thoughtfully. 'Things like the lifeguard's net and the emergency phone. But I'm sure those will be on the wall next to the pool, so you don't need to write that on the poster.'

'There are lots of rules beginning with "no" at swimming pools,' Peanut squeaked. 'Are there any other things little animals shouldn't do?'

'I can't think of anything else at the moment.' Dr KittyCat's bright eyes sparkled. 'Maybe you can make it look a bit more friendly and end with "Have fun!"'

'I'd never have thought of that!' Peanut exclaimed. He added the words with his paintbrush. Then he dipped his tiny paw in the paint pot and made a paw-print border.

'It's the purr-fect poster: informative *and* friendly!' Dr KittyCat told him. 'I'll add my mark at the bottom so everyone knows it's official.'

She carefully added her paw mark to the paper. Then she picked up the poster and pinned it on the clinic wall opposite the door. 'Well done, Peanut. Everyone will see it when they come in.'

Peanut's ears glowed with pride as he washed his paws and wiped a few painty prints off the floor and his tummy. He couldn't wait for the little animals to see his poster! He threw open the clinic door. He could hardly

believe his eyes. For the first time ever,
the waiting room was empty.

'Oh,' he sighed. 'No one's come to
the clinic today!'

'Today is the opening day for the
new pool,' Dr KittyCat reminded him.

'All the little animals are very excited. I expect they'll all be there.'

'But they haven't read my poster yet,' Peanut said worriedly, hopping from foot to foot. 'They might not swim safely!'

'Don't panic, Peanut!' Dr KittyCat told him. 'They'll see it soon. And in the meantime, we can make sure we're ready to rescue.'

'Yes, of course,' said Peanut, sounding a little calmer. 'The notes in the *Furry First-aid Book* are up to date, and the vanbulance is ready to roll,' he added. 'I'll help check your bag while you do your knitting.

It's almost finished, isn't it?'

'Yes!' Dr KittyCat held up her knitting for him to see. Peanut wasn't sure exactly what it was, but it was clear to him that it was approximately mouse sized. Peanut gulped.

'What is it?' he asked nervously.

'A new swimming costume for Pumpkin,' she explained. 'He's growing so fast he will soon have grown out of his old one.'

Phew! thought Peanut. 'I'm sure Pumpkin will love it!' he said. He opened Dr KittyCat's flowery doctor's bag. He had a good idea of its contents, but he wanted to be sure. 'What should be in here?' he asked.

'Stethoscope, ophthalmoscope, thermometer, tweezers, otoscope, tongue depressor, scissors, syringe, surgical headlamp, magnifying glass,' Dr KittyCat murmured, clicking

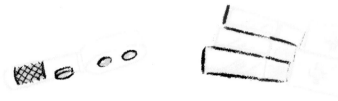

her knitting needles. 'Paw-cleansing
gel, wipes, bandages, tape, gauze,
sticking plasters, instant cool packs,
peppermint lozenges, medicines,
ointments, clinical waste bag . . . and
reward stickers, of course!'

'It's all there,' Peanut said.

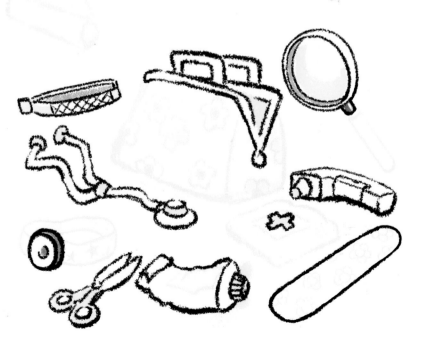

'Put this in, too, please. I've just finished it.' Dr KittyCat handed him the little swimsuit and the leftover ball of wool that she'd speared with her knitting needles. Peanut clicked the flowery doctor's bag closed. He jumped as the old-fashioned telephone on his desk began to ring.

Brring! Brring!

Peanut's heart beat faster as he hauled the heavy handset off its cradle and on to his desk. *It might be an emergency!* he thought. 'Dr KittyCat's clinic. How can we help?' he answered,

speaking into
the mouthpiece.
Then he ran to
the earpiece
to listen to
the reply. The
telephone cord wrapped itself around
his tail.

'Eek!' he squeaked, wriggling out
of the cord. 'Dr KittyCat! Something
has happened at the swimming pool.
A puppy's hurt! They need us! It's an
emergency!'

'Don't panic, Peanut. We're ready
to rescue!' Dr KittyCat took the phone.
'Keep the patient quiet and calm,'

she purred reassuringly. 'We'll be there in a whisker!' And with a swish of her stripy tail, she picked up her bag and headed for the door. Peanut scurried after her as fast as his little legs would go.

Chapter Two

The brightly painted vanbulance was parked outside the clinic. Peanut and Dr KittyCat jumped in and carefully tucked their tails out of the way of the doors and the seat belts.

'Ready to rescue?' Dr KittyCat asked Peanut.

'Ready to rescue!' Peanut pressed

the siren button on
the dashboard, and
Dr KittyCat slammed her
paw on the accelerator.

Nee-nah, nee-nah, nee-nah.

They sped off through Thistletown.
Peanut held on to the dashboard so
tightly that his knuckles went white.

As the vanbulance thundered over the creaky timber bridge, he shut his eyes and tried to think of cheese. The wheels screeched, and the vanbulance tilted. Even with his eyes shut, Peanut knew that they were going round Duckpond Bend! *There's no need to panic,* Peanut told himself. *Dr KittyCat drives fast, but she drives safely.* For a while the road seemed straighter.

Then there was an extra-loud squeal of brakes, and Peanut was thrown to one side as the vanbulance navigated a tight left turn.

'We've reached the swimming pool car park,' Dr KittyCat announced.

Peanut opened his eyes. The car park was full of vehicles of all shapes and sizes. It looked as if the entire population of Thistletown had come to the new pool on opening day.

'There aren't any spaces!' he squeaked. 'Where can we leave the vanbulance?'

'Don't panic, Peanut,' Dr KittyCat said calmly. 'There's always a space for an emergency vehicle outside a public building.' She drove carefully through the car park and pulled the vanbulance into a special parking place in front of the pool.

Peanut sighed with relief as he

turned off the siren. They jumped
out and hurried inside.

In the new changing room,
little animals wearing swimming
costumes were huddled together.

Half of them were dry, but the other half were dripping wet. They all had towels draped around their shoulders, and they looked scared. They were crowding round a very furry, wet little puppy Peanut hadn't seen before.

'Who's that?' Peanut asked Dr KittyCat.

'That's Loganberry—Logan for short,' Dr KittyCat said. 'He's new to Thistletown. He arrived at the same time as Ginger the kitten.'

'They're not in your *Furry First-aid Book*!' Peanut squeaked.

'Their paperwork is in the pile on my desk,' Dr KittyCat explained quickly. 'I looked through it to make sure they didn't need any special care, so I know Logan and Ginger are both very healthy. Neither of them have been to the clinic yet.'

'I'll put them in the *Furry First-aid Book* the minute we get back,' Peanut said.

'Aroo, aroo, aroo!' Logan lifted his muzzle and howled pathetic little howls.

He was sitting in a puddle of water. But why was the water pink?

Peanut gasped. He could feel the panic rising up from his toes. 'Eek!' he squeaked. 'There's blood on the floor. Logan must be bleeding!'

'Don't panic, Peanut,' Dr KittyCat whispered. 'You'll frighten everyone if you do. A first-aider has to be calm in a crisis.'

'Sorry, I forgot for a moment,' Peanut murmured. He took a deep breath. 'Dr KittyCat is here now,' he announced to the small crowd, as much to reassure himself as anyone else. 'There's nothing to be scared of.' And he made sure the other animals moved away to give Dr KittyCat and Logan some space.

Dr KittyCat helped Peanut to wash his paws with soap and water at the sink and then washed her own, too. She knelt down beside Logan.

'It only takes a tiny drop of blood to make a lot of water turn pink,' she said comfortingly. 'My name is Dr KittyCat, and this is my assistant, Peanut. Can you tell us what happened?'

Logan took a deep shuddery breath. 'I . . . I threw open my locker door to get my towel out, and it banged my tail!' he whimpered.

'Let me see.' Dr KittyCat carefully examined Logan's tail and gently ran her paws along it.

'I can feel a tiny bit of swelling in the middle,' she said. 'Can you still wag your tail, Logan?'

Logan gave his tail a little twitch.

'Very good,' Dr KittyCat smiled. 'If there were any fractures, it would be very difficult for you to move your tail. You've bruised it a little, but the skin's not broken. It will feel much better once I put a cool compress on it.'

Peanut took an instant cool pack out of Dr KittyCat's bag. He twisted the bag until he felt the inner bag burst. Then he shook it up and down and side to side until he felt the contents go ice-cold. He handed it to Dr KittyCat.

Dr KittyCat gently pressed the icy pack against the bruised area on Logan's tail. 'Is that a bit better?' she asked Logan.

'A tiny bit.' Logan's shoulders shuddered.

'Where did the blood come from if
it didn't come from Logan's tail?' asked
Peanut, frowning. Then he turned to
the little animals. 'Are you all OK?' he
asked. Everyone nodded their heads.

'W-we're all f-f-fine!' shivered Sage
the owlet. 'W-we're just w-w-worried
about Logan. He's new around here,
so he needs some f-f-f-friends.' Her
beak was chattering so much she could
hardly answer.

'Logan's safe in our paws,'
Dr KittyCat told her. She looked up
at the little animals. 'Some of you are
cold and damp. Go and dry off and get
yourselves nice and warm while we
look after Logan. There will be plenty
of time to make friends later.'

She turned her attention back to
the little puppy.

'Was it only your tail that got
hurt?' she asked, gently lifting Logan's
head to look in his eyes. 'I think the
blood must have come from somewhere
else.'

Logan's scruffy little eyebrows
twitched. He looked away from

Dr KittyCat and began to *aroo, aroo, aroo* again.

'He can't look you in the eyes,' Peanut whispered in Dr KittyCat's furry ear. 'I think he's hiding something. Perhaps he's embarrassed because he didn't get to the toilet in time. That might be a puddle of puppy pee!'

'Yes, it's possible that Logan could have blood in his urine,' Dr KittyCat murmured thoughtfully. 'There was no record of it in his notes, but Logan might be suffering from a bladder infection. They sometimes start suddenly, and they can be very, very painful!'

'Please give Logan some privacy,'
Peanut told the little animals who were
still watching. They slowly backed away.

'It's OK,' Dr KittyCat calmly
whispered in Logan's furry ear. 'You
can show me and Peanut where it really
hurts. We're furry first-aiders. There's
nothing to be ashamed of. Whatever it
is that's wrong, we're here to help make
it right.'

Chapter Three

Logan gave a little howl as he sat up and gingerly shrugged off his thick towel. It was hiding a big, sore-looking graze on his shoulder.

'That's a nasty graze,' Dr KittyCat meowed. She took out her magnifying glass to take a closer look.

'How did you do it?' she asked Logan.

'I forgot to look where I was going when I ran across the car park to the pool,' Logan whimpered. 'I skidded on some loose gravel and fell and grazed my shoulder.'

Dr KittyCat asked Logan more questions about how he fell and whether he had pain anywhere else. She wanted to make sure he hadn't hit his head. 'Your graze looks quite clean because you've been swimming—but swimming pool water is not the best thing for grazes because it has chemicals in it,' she murmured. 'I can see some tiny bits of gravel are still stuck in it, too. We need to clean it properly.'

Peanut knew exactly what to do. He rushed off and came back with a bowl of clean, warm, soapy water. He set the bowl down beside Dr KittyCat and took out the cotton gauze swabs.

Dr KittyCat took one and dipped it into the water. Logan began to wriggle away.

'Dr KittyCat will be very gentle,' Peanut reassured the poorly puppy. 'You need to sit as still as possible.'

Logan gritted his teeth.

'Try to relax and breathe slowly in and out,' Dr KittyCat said soothingly. Logan unclenched his jaw. 'And it's best if you look away while I work,' she added.

'You shouldn't have gone swimming with a graze like that,' Peanut commented as Dr KittyCat calmly and carefully cleaned Logan's graze. *Is there room on my poster to say 'No swimming if you have a bad graze or a cut'?* he wondered.

'I know.' Logan's ears drooped. 'But it wasn't bleeding much, and I really, really wanted to go swimming in the new pool, so I didn't tell anyone. I jumped in before anyone could see.'

'Didn't it hurt too much to swim?' Peanut asked.

'I was too busy swimming to notice!' Logan said. 'It only really started hurting when I got out. I rushed to my locker to get my towel to cover it up, but I was hurrying too much and I banged my tail. Then I started howling, and everyone noticed the blood!'

'Your shoulder must be sore now,' Dr KittyCat said sympathetically.

'It is,' Logan snuffled. 'But you're very kind and gentle, and I know you will make it better. My tail doesn't hurt any more.'

'Good.' Dr KittyCat peered at the graze. 'I need a bit more light on this . . . '

Peanut handed her the surgical headlamp, and she pulled it on over her furry silvery ears.

'There is still a tiny piece of gravel in your graze,' she told Logan. 'I have to get it out so it can heal properly. I'll be as quick and as gentle as I can.'

Peanut handed over a pair of long sterile tweezers. Logan was still looking away.

'It'll soon be over,' Peanut consoled him.

'There!' Dr KittyCat exclaimed. 'The gravel is out, Logan. You've been very brave. I just need you to be brave for a few seconds more while I pat your shoulder dry.'

Peanut held out another cotton gauze swab. Logan winced as Dr KittyCat carefully dabbed at the sore area.

'Well done, Logan. The worst bit is over!' she said cheerfully. 'Now we need to cover the wound with a clean dressing. I don't recall seeing any notes about allergies in your file, Logan. As far as you know, are you OK with sticking plasters?'

Logan nodded. 'We don't have a sticking plaster that's big enough to cover this graze,' Dr KittyCat went on. 'So we'll have to use gau—'

Before she'd finished her sentence, Peanut had opened a new square of sterile gauze and passed it to her.

'A good assistant is a bit like a mind reader,' Dr KittyCat purred. 'And you're a very, very good assistant, Peanut,' she said.

Peanut beamed. He handed her some strips of tape he'd cut to fix the gauze to Logan's fur.

'All done, Logan!' Dr KittyCat got to her feet. 'Thanks for your assistance, Peanut. You've been a great help!'

Peanut couldn't stop smiling as he put the used swabs in Dr KittyCat's clinical waste bag and threw away the instant cool pack. Then he packed away the rest of the medical equipment.

'How do you feel?' Peanut asked Logan as he and Dr KittyCat helped the puppy get slowly to his feet.

'Much better now!' said Logan. His ears looked much perkier, and he gave a tiny twitch of his tail.

'You were very brave when I cleaned your graze, so you deserve a

special sticker!'
Dr KittyCat
said, smiling, as
Peanut got one
out of the bag.

I was a purr-fect patient for Dr KittyCat!

Logan proudly
stuck the 'I was a purr-fect patient for
Dr KittyCat!' sticker on his furry chest.
'Can I go swimming again tomorrow?'
he asked hopefully.

'Not tomorrow, I'm afraid. You
should wait until next week,' Dr
KittyCat told him. 'A bad graze like that
needs a chance to heal.' She gave Logan
a wound aftercare information sheet to
take home with him.

'Next week?' Logan looked very sad. 'I was hoping to come to the pool every day this week so I could get to know everyone and make new friends. I really love swimming, too. It's such fun!'

'That's what Dr KittyCat thinks too,' squeaked Peanut. 'But it sounds a bit scary to me. Maybe it's because I can't swim.'

'You can't swim?' Dr KittyCat sounded shocked. 'Everyone in Thistletown should learn to swim in case they fall into the duck pond!'

'I try to keep away from the duck pond,' Peanut explained. 'I don't like deep water. The closest I get to falling in the duck pond is when the vanbulance goes round Duckpond Bend!'

'I don't intend to drive the vanbulance into the duck pond,'

Dr KittyCat said thoughtfully. 'But you never know. Accidents do happen . . .'

Chapter Four

Sage strutted into the changing room with a list of names. She hooted loudly to get everyone's attention. 'Mrs Hazelnut's first swimming lesson for beginners is about to start,' she announced. She looked at the list. 'Daisy and Ginger the kittens, Nutmeg the guinea pig, Clover the bunny, and

Bramble the hedgehog, please make
your way to the pool.'

Dr KittyCat looked at Peanut.
'What a great opportunity for you to
learn to swim!' she meowed. 'Why
don't you join the beginners' class right
now?'

Me? Swimming? Eek! Peanut
thought. 'I can't go swimming now!'
he squeaked. 'I don't have a swimming
costume!'

Dr KittyCat rummaged in her
flowery doctor's bag and pulled out the
costume she had just finished knitting.
'You could use the one I made for
Pumpkin. He's a bit bigger than you

are, but I think it will work if we pull
up the straps.' She turned to the little
hamster. 'You don't mind, do you,
Pumpkin?'

'Peanut's welcome to use my new costume,' Pumpkin grinned. 'I won't need it for a while. I haven't grown out of my old costume yet.'

Peanut reluctantly pulled on the costume. It was very baggy.

Dr KittyCat took the roll of tape out of her bag and cut off a couple of strips. Then she pulled up the straps on the swimming costume, folded the extra material over, and used the tape to stick it down.

'I haven't got a float,' Peanut squeaked. 'Or armbands.'

'I'll fetch my spare float from my locker. You can use that,' Clover said, hopping off.

'And you can have my armbands. I don't want them. I can swim a bit already,' Ginger meowed proudly.

I need another excuse, quick! Peanut thought as he reluctantly took the float that Clover thrust at him. He looked at the big, air-filled armbands that Ginger was holding.

'A kitten's armbands are much too big for a little mouse,' he said, twitching his tail. 'I'm really sorry, but I won't be able to join in the beginners' swimming lesson after all.'

'You can wear one of Ginger's armbands around your tummy like a swim ring!' Dr KittyCat suggested, placing the armband on the floor in front of Peanut.

Peanut stepped into it and wiggled it up around his tummy. His ears and whiskers began to quiver.

'Cheer up,' Logan woofed. 'It'll be fun! I'll come with you.' He took Peanut by the paw. Dr KittyCat and the little animals followed on.

A footbath full of water blocked their way to the pool area. On the wall beside it there was a notice that read: 'Wash your feet before entering the pool.'

How deep is that water? Peanut

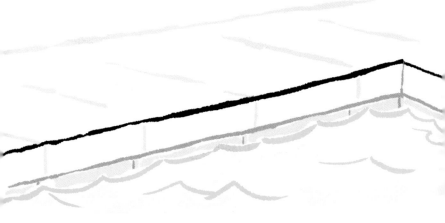

wondered. He stopped at the edge and peered doubtfully into it, still holding Logan's paw. Dr KittyCat lifted up her tail and splashed cheerfully past them. Peanut took a deep breath and let Logan lead him through the shallow water and into the pool area.

There were two pools: a big one for advanced swimmers and a small one for beginners, but even the small pool looked big to Peanut.

Peanut felt as if his tummy was full of butterflies. He watched as Daisy, Nutmeg, Clover, Ginger, and Bramble trotted happily into the beginners' pool and began to splash around and play

with the balls floating in the water.

'Everyone seems to be enjoying it,' Peanut said uncertainly. His legs were beginning to feel a bit shaky.

'They think swimming's fun!' Logan told him. 'And so will you! Come on, Peanut. Put a toe in the water and feel how warm it is. That's all you need to do for a start. Do you need to hold my paw?'

Peanut could see all the other little animals watching him. No one else needed their paws held, he told himself.

'I'll be fine on my own, thanks, Logan!' Peanut took a few shaky steps away from Logan. He was standing on the edge! He peered into the water.

He could see the bottom, but it looked very deep for a little mouse. His knees started to knock together.

'You're doing it!' Logan cheered as Peanut gingerly dipped a toe in the water. But Peanut's legs were so wobbly that he lost his balance! Clover's float flew out of his paws, and he fell head first into the water with a big . . .

SPLASH!

Eek! Peanut opened his mouth to shriek, but he swallowed a great big mouthful of water, and no noise came out. He thrashed his tail. He was really panicking now!

Chapter Five

Peanut floated back up to the surface with Ginger's armband still around his tummy. He spat out the mouthful of water. *Thpppp!* He bobbed up and down and blinked water out of his eyes. There was a loud meow. 'Don't panic, Peanut!' Dr KittyCat called. 'I'm ready to rescue!'

Peanut gasped. An enormous

fishing net was coming towards him! Dr
KittyCat had grabbed the safety net on
the wall and was about to fish him out!

'There's no need for you to worry,
Dr KittyCat!' another voice said
soothingly. 'I'm right here. I've got
you, Peanut.' Peanut felt furry paws
supporting his chin and his tummy.
    'That's it, Peanut. Keep your chin

up and kick your feet.' Mrs Hazelnut
helped Peanut to the side of the pool.

'I'm sorry I panicked, Mrs
Hazelnut,' Dr KittyCat said. 'For a
moment I forgot that you were in charge
of the beginners' swimming lesson.'

She replaced the net in the wall holder. 'Shall I help you out, Peanut?'

Peanut shook his head. The water was lovely and warm, and there were two rescuers at the pool, not one. He was surprised to find that he felt really safe!

'I'll stay in the pool for a bit longer,' he said.

'Go, Peanut, you're a brave little mouse!' Logan cheered from the side.

Peanut felt his ears flush with pride. In no time at all, he was holding on to a float, kicking his feet, and swishing his tail.

'You're doing really well!' Logan

encouraged him on as Peanut splished and splashed his way across the pool.

Peanut felt braver and braver. He didn't even mind that water had got in his ears and up his nose. In fact, he was really disappointed when the lesson ended and Mrs Hazelnut gestured to him to get out. He clambered out of the pool, grinning from ear to ear. His borrowed swimming costume had gone so soggy that the bottom was drooping round his knees.

Dr KittyCat was smiling at him. She seemed to be talking to him, too.

'What did you say?' he asked her.

Dr KittyCat's lips moved again.

'I can't hear you!' Peanut squeaked. His voice sounded to him as if his head was stuck in a big ball of cotton wool. 'Something's wrong with my ears!'

Chapter Six

Dr KittyCat took Peanut's head in her paws and gently tilted it first to one side and then to the other.

Peanut heard a little pop. A drop of water dripped out of one of his big round ears.

'Don't panic, Peanut. You've just got water in your ears,' Dr KittyCat said calmly. 'It sometimes happens after you've been swimming.'

Peanut tilted his head to the other side.

'Any luck?' asked Dr KittyCat. Her voice still sounded a bit muffled.

'My ear isn't clearing!' Peanut squeaked. 'It feels sort of tickly, too. Please can you take a look in it with your otoscope?'

'I'm sure it's just water, Peanut,' Dr KittyCat told him. 'But I'll examine it if it will make you feel better.'

Back in the changing room, Dr KittyCat took out her otoscope. She put on a new hygiene cover, inserted the otoscope gently into Peanut's ear, and clicked on the light beam.

'The inside of your ear looks

completely normal,' she said comfortingly. 'There's no redness or swelling at all.' She threw away the used hygiene cover and returned the otoscope to her bag.

'You're finding it hard to hear out of one ear because a drop of water has got trapped in it,' Dr KittyCat explained.

'It feels really strange,' Peanut groaned. 'If this is what happens after swimming, I don't know if I want to go to the pool any more.'

'It's unlikely to happen very often,' Dr KittyCat purred. 'Try not to worry. The water almost always dries out on its own.'

'Can't I just stick something in my ear, like a cotton bud?' Peanut asked. 'That would dry it out!'

'Never, ever stick anything in your ear,' Dr KittyCat said seriously, 'or anyone else's ear for that matter. You might damage the eardrum. But you can try a few things to get rid of the water.'

'What sort of things?' Peanut asked suspiciously.

'Pull on your ear and gently jiggle it,' Dr KittyCat said.

Peanut grabbed his ear with both paws and waggled it backwards and forwards. 'That's not helping,'

Peanut told her.

'Try yawning,' Dr KittyCat instructed.

Peanut yawned so hard that his jaw clicked. Once he'd started, it was hard to stop.

'That didn't make any difference to the water in my ear,' Peanut said, yawning again. 'It just made me feel tired.'

'Sometimes chewing will clear it. Pretend you're chewing a big block of cheese!' Dr KittyCat suggested.

'I can do that!' Peanut pretended to chew on a big wedge of imaginary Cheddar. When he finished that, he started chewing on a block of imaginary Emmental. He always liked a piece of holey Swiss cheese. The thought of it made him smile, but it didn't help his ear.

'My ear's still blocked,' Peanut
sighed.

'Never mind, Peanut. When we
get back, we can try a gentle blast of
warm air from a hairdryer. And, if the
water hasn't gone away in a day or two,
I can give you some special ear drops to
prevent infection.' Dr KittyCat packed
up her flowery doctor's bag. 'It's time we
were getting back to the clinic.'

*There's a chance
of infection?* Peanut
thought, but before
he could panic, Logan
came up to them.

He was wagging his tail.

'You're looking much happier, Logan!' Dr KittyCat said, smiling. 'Are you feeling better?'

'Much better, thank you!' Logan yapped. 'Mrs Hazelnut noticed me helping Peanut. She says I can come along to the pool every day and help encourage the beginners. I'll be able to make friends here while my tail and graze are healing!'

Peanut and Dr KittyCat waved goodbye to Mrs Hazelnut, Logan, and the little animals, and made their way to the vanbulance. Peanut clambered into the front seat and strapped himself in. His legs and tail felt really tired after his swim and all that yawning. He yawned again as Dr KittyCat put her paw on the accelerator and the vanbulance roared out of the car park. In no time at all they were at Duckpond Bend.

Neee-owww! Peanut was thrown to one side as the vanbulance rounded the bend on two wheels. He heard a tiny pop in his bad ear.

Bump, bump, bump! went the vanbulance over the timber bridge. Peanut felt a drop of water trickle out of his ear.

'My ear's cleared,' he laughed. *I won't get an ear infection now*, he thought with relief. For once he was thankful for Dr KittyCat's fast driving, even if there was a tiny chance that the vanbulance would end up in the duck pond one day.

'I'm happy to hear that,' Dr KittyCat meowed as she parked the vanbulance outside the clinic. 'I was afraid it would put you off swimming.'

'I've decided to go back to the pool

for more lessons after all,' Peanut told her. 'One day, I might need to know how to swim!' He opened the clinic door.

The 'Swim safe!' poster was the first thing they saw as they went in.

'It's a good poster,' Peanut squeaked, 'but I have to add some things.' He fetched a fat felt-tip pen from the pot on his desk and squeezed in the words 'or car park' so that the first line read 'No running in the pool area or car park.' Then he fitted in another couple of lines that said: 'Be careful when you open and close the locker doors.' and 'Don't go swimming if you have a bad graze or cut.'

'Now it really is purr-fect!' purred Dr KittyCat.

Peanut sat down at his desk and took out the *Furry First-aid Book*.

'I need to put Logan and Ginger in the book and write up the notes on Logan,' he said, 'and learn more about how to care for my ears.'

'It's very important to care for your ears, whatever shape or size they may be,' Dr KittyCat agreed. She opened her bag and took out her knitting needles and the leftover ball of wool. She turned to him and smiled.

'Now that you've decided to get your ears wet again at Mrs Hazelnut's next lesson, I shall knit you your very own swimsuit!'

Peanut's ears quivered. 'That's er . . . that's very kind!' he squeaked.

The end

Dr KittyCat's top ten tips for first-aiders

1. Take care! Don't become a casualty yourself!

2. Stay calm.

3. Prioritise: what is the most important illness or injury to deal with first?

4. Listen to your casualty (and their friends or family).

5. Be positive and reassuring.

6. Remember to get help when you can: two heads are better than one!

7. Write important things down so you can tell the doctor or ambulance without forgetting something.

8. Sometimes you might not have your first aid kit, so improvise with what you do have.

9. Remember the most painful injury (or the loudest patient) might not be the most important.

10. Above all, remember that whatever you do should be to make the patient better, or stop them getting worse.

If you loved Logan the Puppy, here's an extract from another Dr KittyCat adventure:

Dr KittyCat is ready to rescue: Pumpkin the Hamster

This time Dr KittyCat is helping a hamster called Pumpkin who takes a tumble on a stargazing evening . . .

Peanut took a deep breath. 'I'm a furry first-aider,' he told himself. 'I can't let Pumpkin and Dr KittyCat down.'

His paws shook as he took off his mittens and pulled on Pumpkin's headlamp.

'Shine your torches here,' he squeaked.

The little animals focused beams

of light on the hole. Peanut could see
tiny tree roots poking out the sides,
like a mass of wriggly worms. Peanut
gulped. His heart thumped wildly
as he scrambled down the
peaty sides of the hole. But
the instant he was beside
Pumpkin, he forgot to be
scared of the dark.
He was ready to
rescue.

Here are some other stories that we think you'll love!

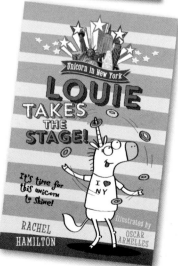